Martin on the Moon

Owlkids Books Inc.
10 Lower Spadina Avenue, Suite 400, Toronto, Ontario M5V 2Z2
www.owlkids.com

Published in Quebec under the title *Xavier-la-lune* © 2010
Dominique et compagnie Québec, a division of Éditions Héritage Inc. Quebec, Canada J4R 1K5
www.dominiqueetcompagnie.com

Distributed in Canada by University of Toronto Press
5201 Dufferin Street, Toronto, Ontario M3H 5T8

Distributed in the United States by Publishers Group West
1700 Fourth Street, Berkeley, California 94710

Library and Archives Canada Cataloguing in Publication

Audet, Martine, 1961-
[Xavier-la-lune. English]
    Martin on the moon / by Martine Audet ; illustrated by
Luc Melanson ; translated by Sarah Quinn.

Translation of: Xavier-la-lune.
ISBN 978-1-926973-16-6

    I. Melanson, Luc II. Quinn, Sarah
III. Title: Xavier-la-lune. English.

PS8551.U374X3813 2012   jC843'.54   C2011-905823-5

Library of Congress Control Number: 2011935960

  Canadian Patrimoine
Heritage canadien

 Canada

 Ontario
Ontario Media Development
Corporation

Canada Council Conseil des Arts
for the Arts du Canada

ONTARIO ARTS COUNCIL
CONSEIL DES ARTS DE L'ONTARIO

Société de développement
de l'industrie des médias
de l'Ontario

We acknowledge the financial support of the Canada Council for the Arts, the Ontario Arts Council, the
Government of Canada through the Canada Book Fund (CBF) and the Government of Ontario through
the Ontario Media Development Corporation's Book Initiative for our publishing activities.

Manufactured by WKT Co. Ltd.
Manufactured in Shenzhen, Guangdong, China, in October 2011
Job #11CB2492

A   B   C   D   E   F

 Publisher of Chirp, chickaDEE and OWL
www.owlkids.com

Martin on the Moon

Written by Martine Audet
Illustrated by Luc Melanson

Owl kids

My name is Martin.
I wonder what their names are...
If the girl in front of me had braids,
she would look just like my friend Athena.

I wonder what the teacher's name is...
She has gray hair the same color as my cat Happy.
And she has pink cheeks, just like Mum Mum.
But she doesn't have Mum Mum's big smile.

Mum Mum's smile is as wide as the river...

Last summer she borrowed Uncle Abel's car
and we drove and drove (so much that I got
a little carsick and we had to stop twice
for bathroom breaks and sandwiches).

The river is so far away, so beautiful.
It's not like the empty blackboard behind the teacher.
It's huge and full of water!

Water that swishes, water that splashes,
water that nibbles at the sand and the rocks
and then spits them out as seaweed and
silky smooth pebbles and little blue shells
that break if you're not careful.

The river is always changing.
Sometimes it's as smooth as glass,
and if you have binoculars
you can see seals in the water.
Sometimes it swells and roars and smells yucky.
It's almost scary.
The kind of scary that makes you shiver a little or
laugh a little, with your hands covering your eyes.
Scared giggles, silly giggles, like my friend
Athena's giggles.
I love her butterfly giggles!
Once I almost caught one with my camera!

But today is the first day of school,
and I'm here to learn.

To learn the alphabet, the letters A B C...
I also have to learn numbers.
That's why I need to concentrate in class.
No walking on the moon today.

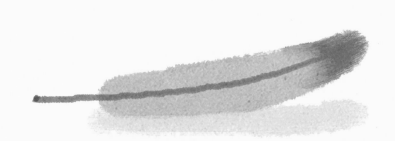

I concentrate really hard, but the blackboard
is still empty.
The teacher is waving her arms around, talking
with her hands.
She looks like one of those seagulls that flies
along the riverbanks, or one of those other birds
that sits on the rocks waiting for its wings to dry.
They cry out, they play in the air, and then
suddenly they dive down to catch fish.

I miss those times.
I miss the waves and the wind.
I even miss the rain.

Once, I was outside drawing a tree
when all of a sudden, BOOOOOM!
The sky cracked!
The noise made me jump
and color outside the lines.
Then it started raining,
so I ran back to the cottage
as fast as I could go.
My drawing got a little wet, but
I showed it to Mum Mum anyway.

"When it rains, it looks like someone is coloring
in the sky and going outside the lines," I said.

"What a beautiful image!" Mum Mum exclaimed.
"I'm going to put it in a poem."

Mum Mum writes lots of poems.
She puts together words that paint pictures
in your mind and make music in your heart.

Mum Mum explained to me that poems help
you put things into words that are painful or
wonderful or that you just don't understand.

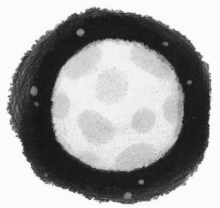

"A lot of people think that
poems are silly," Mum Mum told me.
"But actually, they're like kisses, tiny little
nothings that mean so much!"
Oh, it would be so sad not to have kisses!
Butterfly kisses, scraped-knee kisses...

Suddenly I notice the whole class is staring at me.

"Where are you, Martin? On the moon?"
asks the teacher. "Who are you blowing kisses to?"

I blush right to the tips of my ears,
but the teacher is smiling a big smile,
a smile as wide as the river.

I hold on really tight to a smooth pebble
from my vacation that I keep in my pocket.
Then I think of the poem that I wrote with
Mum Mum.

Tiny pebble,
Small as sand,

From the beach,
In my hand.

Tiny pebble,
In my hand,

From the beach,
From the sand.

The redness in my cheeks goes away and I start
telling everyone about the waves in the river
and how they kiss the riverbanks, and about
Mum Mum's kisses, and the other kisses
that I miss, like the kisses from my cat Happy,
who died last summer...

So the teacher, whose name is Ms. Fisher,
teaches us how to draw kisses.
Then we tape them up on the big, empty
blackboard, with letters for our names, the names
of all the friends in my class:
Elias, Rose, Mei, Irena, Gertrude, Malek, Sebastian,
Chloe, Vincent, Scarlett, Mariko, Oliver, Amy,
Beatrice, Nadia, Alice, Anthony, Savannah-Lou,
and...

...and me, Martin on the Moon.